Floppy sniffed around their legs – the girls were standing right in front of his kennel and he couldn't get in to warm himself up!

Anneena thought that Biff could come and help tidy her room, but Biff was getting cross – she wanted to play.

'Why should I do something for you, if you won't do anything for me?' she asked.

Floppy shook his head. I wish they'd both do something for *me*, he thought. Get out of my way!

The key on Floppy's collar started to glow.

Suddenly, Biff, Anneena, and Floppy were sucked into a vortex of sparkling colours and lights. They were whizzing round and round, faster and faster . . .

The Magic Key

Tumbleweed Desert

OXFORD
UNIVERSITY PRESS

The children were out in the Robinsons' garden. It was freezing!

'Let's play tag – that'll warm us up,' suggested Biff.

But Chip and Kipper were too cold and went indoors. Anneena was cold too. 'I've got to go home and tidy my room,' she told Biff.

When they landed, Biff, Anneena, and Floppy looked around them and shivered. They were in the middle of a desert, but it was covered in snow. They could hear some lively music, so they ran through the snow to find out where it was coming from.

They met three musicians: Jose, Juan, and Maria.

'Have you come to help us?' asked Juan.

'Tumbleweed Desert is covered in snow,' said Jose.

Maria began to cry. 'The famous family Moochachas who live only to dance are too cold to move!' she sobbed.

Anneena shivered. 'How long has it been this cold?' she asked.

'It started when the weather man got sad!' said Jose.

'When Mickey Gringone stopped smiling, the sun went out and the snow came,' continued Juan.

Biff, Anneena, and Floppy went to visit Mickey Gringone, and sure enough, he looked very gloomy.

'In the old days, the Moochachas came to entertain me,' Mickey told them. 'They danced and told me stories. Then they stopped coming...'

Anneena looked at Biff.

'Why don't *we* tell him a story?' she whispered.

So Biff cleared her throat, and began her story.

'Once upon a time, there was a man called Enrico, who made the best castanets in South America,' she said. 'Everybody wanted Enrico's brilliant castanets but he only made twenty pairs a year.'

'Only twenty pairs!' cried Mickey. 'Why?'

Biff continued her story, explaining that the secret behind Enrico's great castanets was the olive oil he used to grease them. This oil came from olive trees that danced. But whenever he tried to take the oil, the trees ran away, so he could only collect enough for twenty pairs of castanets.

'Then, one day, disaster struck!' said Biff.

'What disaster?' asked Mickey. He was so excited that he smiled – and the sun came out from behind the clouds.

Biff spotted Floppy asleep in Mickey's hammock. This gave her an idea for her story.

'Enrico's old dog, Floppo, fell ill,' she said. 'The vet said the only thing that would save the dog, was the olive oil from the dancing trees mixed with gravy!'

'I got it,' said Mickey, jumping up. 'The old guy gives the pooch all the olive oil!'

'That's right,' replied Biff. 'As soon as Floppo ate the olive oil, he was cured.'

'Brilliant!' said Mickey.

By now, Mickey was so happy that the sun was shining brightly and the snow and ice had begun to melt.

But Mickey wanted to hear more about Enrico. 'What happens next?' he asked.

Biff didn't know what to say. 'Er . . . er . . . I don't know,' she replied. 'No more story?' asked Mickey, with a sad look. Almost at once the sun went in and the clouds gathered. 'Oh, my heart grows cold,' he said. And suddenly, the temperature dropped.

It began to get colder . . . and colder.

Biff turned to Anneena. 'Do something!' she cried.

'Just keep talking, Biff. I'll be right back!' Anneena promised, and off she went.

Biff tried to carry on, but it was getting even colder and her story was getting very silly indeed. If only she could get Mickey to smile again . . .

Then, much to Biff's delight, Anneena arrived back followed closely by the Moochachas, who started singing and dancing.

Mickey beamed. 'Moochachas!' he cried. 'Oh, I've missed you so much!'

Mickey was happy again, and the sun came out once more.

But Anneena was still worried. 'How can you make sure you keep Mickey smiling?' she asked the Moochachas.

Juan grinned. 'No problem! The Moochachas will come and entertain Mickey every day!'

'YEAHHH!' they all cheered, and everyone danced.

Maria handed Anneena a pair of castanets.

'These are for you,' she said.

'Oh, thank you,' Anneena smiled happily. Then she noticed Floppy's collar. 'The key's glowing,' she said.

We're going, thought Floppy.

They were back in the Robinsons' garden, and it was still freezing cold!

'I'm really hot from all that dancing,' said Anneena, clicking her castanets. But Biff's teeth were chattering.

'Let's go to your house and tidy your room,' she suggested. 'At least it'll be warm inside!'

As the girls walked away, Floppy gave a sigh of relief. Now he could get back in his kennel where it was nice and warm.

Home at last! he thought, and he snuggled down to sleep.

OXFORD
UNIVERSITY PRESS

Great Clarendon Street, Oxford OX2 6DP

Oxford University Press is a department of the University of Oxford.
It furthers the University's objective of excellence in research, scholarship,
and education by publishing worldwide in

Oxford   New York

Auckland Cape Town Dar es Salaam Hong Kong Karachi
Kuala Lumpur Madrid Melbourne Mexico City Nairobi
New Delhi Shanghai Taipei Toronto

With offices in

Argentina Austria Brazil Chile Czech Republic France Greece
Guatemala Hungary Italy Japan Poland Portugal Singapore
South Korea Switzerland Thailand Turkey Ukraine Vietnam

Oxford is a registered trade mark of Oxford University Press in the UK and in certain other countries

British Library Cataloguing in Publication Data available
ISBN-13: 978-019-272654-4
ISBN-10: 0-19-272654-4
3 5 7 9 10 8 6 4 2
Printed in China